HANS CHRISTIAN ANDERSEN

Illustrations by *Marcia Brown*

NEW YORK

CHARLES SCRIBNER'S SONS

The Wild Swans

Translated by M. R. JAMES

TO MY MOTHER AND FATHER

Far away from here, in the lands the swallows fly to when we are having winter, there lived a King who had eleven sons and one daughter, Elisa. The eleven brothers, princes they were, went to school with stars on their breasts and swords at their sides. They wrote on gold slates with diamond pencils and could read backwards as easily as forwards. Anybody could see straight off that they were princes. Their sister Elisa sat at home on a little stool made of looking-glass and had a picture book that had cost half the kingdom to buy.

Ah, those children had a fine time of it, to be sure; but it wasn't to be like that forever.

Their father, who was King of the whole country, married a bad Queen, and she was not at all nice to the poor children—the very first day they noticed it. There were great doings all over the palace, and the children played at visitors; but instead of their having all the cakes and baked apples that were left, she only gave them sand in a teacup and told them they could pretend it was something real.

The week after, she boarded the little sister Elisa out in the country with some labourers, and it wasn't long before she got the King to believe such things about the poor princes that he cared not a rap about them any more.

"Fly away out into the world, and fend for yourselves," said the wicked Queen, "fly as big birds without any voice." But she couldn't do all the harm she would have dearly liked to do, and they turned into eleven beautiful wild swans. With a strange cry they flew out of the palace windows, far away over the fields and woods.

11

It was still quite early morning when they passed the place where their sister Elisa lay asleep in the labourer's room. There they hovered over the roof and turned their long necks hither and thither and flapped their wings, but nobody heard or saw it. They had to go on, far upward towards the clouds, far out into the wide world. They flew into a great dark forest that stretched right down to the seashore.

Poor little Elisa, in the labourer's cottage, played with a green leaf—the only toy she had, and she pricked a hole in the leaf and peeped up through it towards the sun, and it seemed as if she was looking at the bright eyes of her brothers. And every time the warm rays shone on her cheek, she thought of all the kisses they had given her.

One day passed just like another; when the breeze
blew through the great rose bushes outside the house, it
whispered to the roses: "Who can be prettier than you?"
But the roses shook their heads and said: "Why, Elisa!"
And when the old woman sat in the doorway, of a Sun-
day, and read her hymn book, the breeze would turn the
leaves and say to the book: "Who can be better than
you?" "Why, Elisa!" said the hymn book. And what the
roses and the hymn book said was no more than the truth.

When she was fifteen years old, she was sent for to go home—and when the Queen saw how pretty she was, she

became full of anger and hatred for her. She would have dearly liked to turn her into a wild swan like her brothers, but that she dared not do at once, for the King wanted to see his daughter.

Early in the morning the Queen went into the bathroom, which was built of marble and decked out with soft skins and lovely rugs, and she took three toads and kissed them and said to the first: "Hop on to Elisa's head when she gets into the bath, that she may become as stupid as you. Sit yourself on her forehead," said she to the second, "that she may become as ugly as you, so that her father shall not know her. Lie on her heart," she whispered to the third, "let her have an evil mind, and let her suffer anguish from it." Then she put the toads into the clear water, which forthwith took on a greenish tint, and called Elisa

and undressed her and made her go down
into the water; and as she dived into it,
the first toad clambered into her hair, and
the second on to her forehead, and the
third on to her heart; but Elisa seemed
not to notice it. At the moment when
she stood up, there were three red
poppies floating on the water.
Had the beasts not been poisonous
and not been kissed by the witch,
they would have been changed into red
roses. Still, flowers they did become,
merely from resting on her head and
her heart. She was too good
and innocent for any witchcraft
to have power over her.

When the wicked Queen saw that, she rubbed Elisa
all over with walnut juice, so that she was all dark brown,
and she smeared her pretty face with a nasty ointment,
and let her lovely hair get all in a tangle. It was impossible
to recognize that pretty Elisa; and so when her father saw
her he was dreadfully shocked and said that was never his
daughter. And indeed nobody knew her but the watch-
dog and the swallows, and they were poor dumb creatures that couldn't do anything.

Poor Elisa! She cried and she thought of her eleven brothers, all gone! Sorrowfully she stole out of the palace and walked all day over field and moor, into the great forest. She had no notion where she wanted to go, but she was in such trouble, and yearned so for her brothers, who, she was sure, had been driven out into the wide world like herself, and she was set on trying to find them.

23

Only a short while had she been in the forest before the night fell. She had wandered far from any road or path, so she laid herself down on the soft moss, said her evening prayer, and rested her head against a stump. All was quiet, the air was very soft, and round about in the grass and moss there shone, like a green fire, hundreds of glowworms. When she gently stirred a twig with her hand, the shining creatures fell down beside her like shooting stars.

All night long she dreamt of her brothers. They were playing together again as children, writing with the diamond pencils on the gold slates, and looking at the lovely picture book that had cost half the kingdom. But on the slates they didn't write as they used to do—noughts and crosses—no, but the bravest of deeds that they had done and all that they had lived through and seen. And in the picture book everything was alive; the birds sang, and the people came out of the book and talked to Elisa and her brothers. But when she turned the page, they jumped back again at once, so as not to cause confusion in the pictures.

When she woke up, the sun was already high. She could not actually see it, for the tall trees spread their branches thick and close; but the rays played through

them like a glittering cloth of gold. There was a fragrance
from the fresh greenwood, and the birds were almost
ready to perch on her shoulders. She heard a splashing of
water. There were a number of springs, all falling into a
pool that had the most beautiful sandy bottom. True, the
bushes grew thick about it, but in one place the deer had
made a wide opening, and there Elisa went to the water,
which was so clear that if the breeze had not so stirred
the branches and bushes that they moved, she
would have thought they were painted on the
bottom of the pool, so sharply was every leaf
reflected there, alike those that the sun shone
through and those that were in the
deepest shadow.

As soon as she saw her own face she was quite horri-fied, so brown and ugly it was; but when she wetted her little hand and rubbed her eyes and forehead, the white skin gleamed out once more. So she laid aside all her clothes and slipped out into the cool water. A fairer King's daughter than she there was not in all the world.

When she had dressed herself again, and plaited her long hair, she went to the spouting spring and drank from the hollow of her hand, and so wandered further into the forest without knowing whither she went. She thought about her brothers, and she thought about the good God who certainly would not forsake her. It was He who made the wild apples grow to feed the hungry; it was He who guided her to a tree of them, its boughs bending under the fruit. And there she made her midday meal and set props under the branches, and then went on into the darkest part of the forest.

It was so still there that she could hear her own foot-steps, nay, every little withered leaf that bent beneath her feet; not a bird was to be seen, not a sunbeam could pierce between the many close-set branches. The tall trunks stood so close together that when she looked straight be-fore her, it seemed as though there was one great fence of timber, trunk after trunk, closing her in all round; yes, indeed, there was a solitude here, the like of which she had never known.

The night was very dark; not a single little glowworm shone out of the moss, and with a troubled mind she lay down to sleep; and then she thought that the branches above her parted and Our Lord looked down on her with loving eyes, and the little angels peeped out above His head and beneath His arms.

When she woke in the morning she was not sure whether she had dreamt it or whether it really had happened.

She walked on
but a few steps,
and then she met
an old woman
with a basket
of berries, some of
which she gave her.
Elisa asked her if
she had not seen
eleven princes
riding through
the forest

"No," said the old woman, "but yesterday I saw eleven swans, with gold crowns on their heads, swimming down the river close by here." And she guided Elisa some way further to a high bank, at the bottom of which was a winding stream. The trees on its banks stretched their long leafy branches across it towards each other, and where their natural growth did not let them meet they had torn their roots loose from the earth and leant over the water and twined their boughs together.

Elisa said goodbye to the old woman, and walked along the stream to the place where it flowed out, on the broad open seashore. All the beautiful sea lay spread out before the young girl, and not a sail showed itself, not a boat was to be seen. How could she get further? She gazed at the numberless pebbles on the beach. The water had worn every one of them round. Glass, iron, stone, everything that lay washed up there had taken its shape from the water, and yet the water was far softer than her own delicate hand. "It keeps rolling on, untiring, and that is how it shapes the hard things smooth, and I will be as

untiring as it is. I thank you for your lesson, you clear rolling billows. One day, my heart tells me, you will bear me
to my brothers."

On the seaweed that had been washed up lay eleven
swans' feathers. She gathered them into a bunch; there
were drops of water on them: whether dew or tears, who
could tell? It was lonely down there on the shore, but she
did not feel it, for the sea gave her infinite changes to look
at, more within a few hours' space than a freshwater lake
would show in a whole year.

If a big black cloud came over, it was as if
the sea would say: "I too can look black." Then
the wind blew and the waves showed their white
sides; but if the clouds shone red, and the wind fell to
sleep, then the sea was like a rose leaf. Sometimes it was
green, sometimes white; but however still it slept there
was always a gentle movement along the beach; the water
heaved, softly as the breast of a sleeping child.

Just as the sun was about to set, Elisa saw eleven wild
swans, with golden crowns on their heads, flying towards
the land. They floated one behind the other, looking like
a long white ribbon. Elisa clambered up the bank and hid
behind a bush. The swans alighted close to her, and
flapped their great white wings.

The moment the sun was beneath the waves the swans' skins fell off and there stood eleven fair princes, Elisa's brothers. She uttered a loud cry, for though they were greatly altered she knew that it was they—was sure it must be they—and she sprang into their arms, and called them by their names. And happy were they when they saw and recognized their little sister, now so tall and so beautiful. They laughed and wept, and very quickly they came to know about each other, and how ill their stepmother had dealt with them all.

"We brothers," said the eldest, "fly about in the shape of wild swans so long as the sun is in the sky; when it is set we take our human shape. So at sunset we must always take care to have a resting place for our feet; for if we were flying then, up among the clouds, we should fall in man's form down into the deep. We do not live here; a fair land like this lies on the other side of the water, but the way to it is long. We have to cross the wide sea, and there is no island on our course where we could spend the night. There is only a little lonely rock that stands up, halfway out, it's only large enough for us to stand side by side and rest on it; if the sea is high, the water leaps up high above us, yet we thank God for it. There we spend the night in our human form; but for it we could never visit our dear fatherland, for our flight takes up two of the

longest days in the year. Only once a year is it permitted
to us to visit our father's home. Eleven days we can stay
here: we fly over this great forest, and from there we can
look at the castle where we were born and where our
father lives, and see the bell tower of the church where our
mother is buried. Here we feel the very trees and bushes

are an heirloom; here the wild horses gallop over the plains as we saw them in our childhood. Here the charcoal burner sings the old songs we danced to as children. Here is our father's land, here we grew up, and here we have found you, you dear little sister. We have still two days to stay here, and then we must away over the sea, to a land that is beautiful, but is not our own. How can we take you with us? We have neither ship nor boat."

"How can I contrive to free you?" said their sister. And they went on talking together almost all night, with only an hour or two of sleep. Elisa was wakened by the sound of swans' wings rustling above her. The brothers were changed once more, and flew about in wide circles, and at last flew away; but one of them, the youngest, stayed behind. The swan laid his head on her bosom and she fondled his white wings; they spent the whole day together. Towards evening the others came back, and when the sun was down, they stood there in their proper forms.

"Tomorrow we fly away from here, and dare not come back for nearly a whole year; but we cannot leave you like this. Have you the courage to come with us? My arm is strong enough to carry you through the forest, and must we not together have strong enough wings to fly with you over the sea?"

"Yes, take me with you," said Elisa.

They spent the whole night in weaving a net out of the
pliant willow bark and stout reeds, and it was large and
strong. On it Elisa lay down, and when the sun came up
and the brothers changed into wild swans, they gripped
the net in their beaks and flew high up towards the clouds,
with their dear sister, who was still asleep. The sunbeams
fell hotly on her face, so one of the swans flew above her
head, that his broad wings might shade her.

46

They were far from land when Elisa awoke. She thought
she was still dreaming, so strange it seemed to her to be
borne over the sea, high through the air. At her side lay a
branch with beautiful ripe berries on it, and a bundle of
sweet-tasting roots. Her youngest brother had gathered
them and laid them by her; and she smiled gratefully at
him, for she knew it was he who was flying straight over
her head and shading her with his wings.

47

They were so high up that the first
ship they saw beneath them looked like a
white gull lying on the water. A great cloud came
behind them, like a mighty mountain, and on it
Elisa saw the shadows of herself and of the
eleven swans, flying there as huge as giants.
It was like a drawing, prettier than any
she had seen before; but as the sun climbed
higher and the cloud was left farther behind,
the moving shadow-picture disappeared. All
day they flew on like a rushing dart through the air,
yet their pace was slower than at other times, now that
they had their sister to carry. Bad weather, too, came
on, and evening grew near. With terror Elisa saw the sun
sinking, and yet the lonely rock in the sea was not in sight. She
thought the swans were playing their wings more strongly. Ah! it

was her fault that they could not go swiftly enough; when the sun was down, they would turn into men and fall into the sea and be drowned! From the very bottom of her heart she sent up a prayer to Our Lord; but still she could see no rock. The black cloud drew nearer, the heavy gusts of wind portended a storm. The clouds gathered into a single huge menacing billow which sped onward, looking like a mass of lead. One flash of lightning followed hard on another.

The sun was now at the very rim of the sea. Elisa's heart beat quickly then; the swans plunged downward so quickly that she thought she must fall, but then they floated again. The sun was half beneath the water. Then first she sighted the little rock beneath her, looking no larger than a seal's head sticking up above the water. How swiftly the sun sank! It was no bigger than a star. Then her foot touched the firm ground and the sun went out like the last spark on a bit of burning paper. She saw her brothers standing about her, but there was no room for any more than them and herself. The sea beat against the rock and burst over them like a shower of rain, the heavens shone with a blaze that kept flaring out, and the thunder rolled, peal on peal; but the sister and the brothers held each other's hands and sang a hymn, and it brought them comfort and courage.

At dawn the air was clear and still, and so soon as the
sun was up, the swans flew off with Elisa from the islet.
The sea was still rough, and when they were high up in
the air it looked as if the white foam on the dark green sea
were millions of swans floating on the water.

When the sun rose higher, Elisa
saw ahead of her, half-swimming in
the air, a range of mountains with
shining masses of ice on their slopes,
and in the midst of it there lay,
stretched out, a palace—
a good mile long—with
one mighty colonnade rising over another.
Low down before it waved groves of palms and
wonderful blossoms, large as mill wheels. She asked if
that were the land she was bound for, but the swans
shook their heads; for that which she was looking at
was the lovely ever-changing cloud palace of the fairy Morgana,
and into it they dared bring no mortal. Elisa gazed upon it.
Suddenly, mountains, groves and palace all fell to pieces, and in
their place rose a score of noble churches, each like the
next, all with lofty towers and pointed windows. She fancied

53

she could hear the organ sounding, but it was the sea she heard. And now she was quite near the churches, but they changed into a fleet of ships sailing onward beneath her. She looked down, and it was but the sea wrack that was spreading over the water. Yes, it was an endless series of changes that she had to look at; but now she saw the real land she was bound for. There rose the beautiful blue mountains, with forests of cedar and towns and castles. Long ere the sun had set she was seated on the slope before a large cave, whose mouth was grown over with delicate green creeping plants that seemed like broidered carpets. "Now we shall see what you dream of here to-night," said the youngest brother, as he led her to her sleeping chamber.

"If I could but dream how to free you!" said she; and
the thought filled her mind most vividly, and earnestly
did she pray to God for His help—nay, even in her sleep

she went on praying. And then it seemed to her that she flew high up into the air, to the cloud palace of the fairy Morgana; and the fairy came to meet her, all beautiful and shining, but all the same, very like the old woman who had given her berries in the forest and told her of the swans with the golden crowns.

"Your brothers can be freed," said she, "but have you courage and endurance? True it is that the sea is softer than your delicate hands, and yet can change the shape of hard stones. But it does not feel the pain that your fingers will feel; it has no heart, and does not suffer the fear and trouble that you must go through. Do you see this stinging nettle that I hold in my hand? Many of this kind grow about the cave where you are sleeping, but only they and those that grow out of churchyard graves are fit for your purpose. Mark you that! These you must pick, though they will burn your skin into blisters. You must break them up with your feet, and you will get flax from them, and with it you must weave and hem eleven shirts with long sleeves. Cast these over the eleven wild swans, and the spell will be broken. But remember this well: that from the moment you begin this work, and until it is wholly ended, even though a year should pass in the meantime, you must not speak. The first word you utter will pierce the heart of your brothers like a deadly dagger.

On your tongue hangs their life. Take good heed of these things." And at the same moment she touched her hand with the nettle; it was like a scorching flame. Elisa awoke with the touch. It was bright day, and close by where she had slept lay a nettle like that which she had seen in her dream. She fell on her knees and gave thanks to God, and went out of the cave to begin her work. With her delicate hands she grasped the horrible nettles, which were like fire to touch, and burnt great blisters on her hands and arms, but she suffered that gladly, if she might but free her dear brothers. She crushed every nettle with her bare feet and wound up the green flax from it.

When the sun was down the brothers came, and were terrified at finding her so silent. They thought it must be a fresh spell cast by that wicked stepmother; but when they saw her hands they understood what she was doing for their sake, and the youngest brother wept, and where his tears fell she felt no more pain, and the burning blisters vanished.

All night she spent on her work, for she could have no rest till she had freed the beloved brothers. All the next day, while the swans were away, she sat in solitude; but the time had never flown so quickly. One shirt was finished, and she set to work on the second.

Just then a hunting horn rang out among
the hills. She was stricken with fear; the sound
came nearer. She heard the baying of hounds.
In terror she took refuge in the cave, and tied
the nettles she had gathered and hackled into a
bundle, and seated herself on it.

A great hound came leaping from among
the bushes—and another just after it, and yet
another. They bayed aloud and ran forward and
then back again. Before many minutes had
passed the whole band of hunters were
outside the cave, and the handsomest
of them was the King of the country.
He advanced towards Elisa.
Never had he beheld
a fairer maid.

"How came you here, you beautiful child?"
said he. Elisa shook her head, she dared not speak,
the saving of her brothers, nay, their
life was at stake; and she hid her
hand beneath her apron, that
the King might not see
what she was suffering.

"Come with me," said he, "you must not stop here. If you are as good as you are beautiful I will dress you in silks and velvets, and put a golden crown on your head, and you shall have your home in the finest of my palaces." And with that he lifted her up on his horse. She wept and wrung her hands. But the King said: "I only desire your happiness; one day you will thank me."

And so off he rode among the mountains, holding her before him on his horse, and the huntsmen followed.

At sunset the fair city with its churches and domes lay
before them; and the King led her into the palace where
great fountains plashed in the lofty marble halls, and
walls and roof glowed with paintings; but she had no
eyes for that; she wept and sorrowed. Listlessly she al-
lowed the women to dress her in royal apparel, twine
pearls in her hair, and put delicate gloves upon her
blistered hands.

When at last she stood arrayed in all her splendour, she was so dazzlingly beautiful that all the court bowed deep and low before her, and the King chose her for his bride. Yet the Archbishop shook his head and muttered that this pretty wood-maiden was surely a witch who had dazzled their eyes, and corrupted the heart of the King.

But the King would not listen to that. He made the music ring out, and the costliest dishes be served, and the fairest girls dance about her, and she walked through fragrant gardens into splendid halls; but not a smile came to her lips or into her eyes. Sorrow stood there, the perpetual heir and possessor. But now the King opened a

little chamber, hard by the place where she was to sleep. It was decked with costly green hangings, and was just

like the cave she had been in. On the floor lay the bundle of flax she had spun from the nettles, and from the ceiling hung the shirt that had already been woven. All this, one of the huntsmen had brought with him as a curiosity.

"Here you can dream yourself back in your old home," said the King, "here is the work you were busying yourself with. Now in the midst of all your splendour it will amuse you to remember that old time."

When Elisa saw this, which lay so near her heart, a smile played about her mouth, and the colour came back into her cheeks at the thought of the saving of her brothers, and she kissed the King's hand and he pressed her to his heart, and bade all the church bells proclaim the wedding festival. The lovely dumb girl from the forest was to be Queen of all the land.

The Archbishop whispered slanderous words into the ear of the King, but they did not make their way to his heart. The bridal was to be. The Archbishop himself had to set the crown on her head, and he spitefully pressed down the narrow ring upon her brow so that it hurt her, yet a heavier ring lay about her heart—sorrow for her brothers. She hardly felt the bodily pain. Her mouth was dumb, for a single word would end her brothers' life, but

in her eyes there lay a deep affection for this handsome
King who did everything to make her happy. With her
whole heart, she grew more loving towards him day by
day. Oh, if she could but confide in him and tell him of
her suffering! but dumb she must remain, in dumbness
must she finish her task. So at night she would steal from
his side and go into the little room apart, that was decked
out like the cave, and weave one shirt after another. But
when she began on the seventh she had no flax left.

In the churchyard, she knew, grew the nettles she must use; but she had to gather them herself. How was she to get there?

"Oh, what is the pain in my fingers to the suffering in my heart," she thought. "I must risk it! Our Lord will not let me fall out of His hands." With a pain at her heart as if it were a crime she was plotting, she stole down to the garden, in the bright moonlight night, and went along the long avenues out into the empty streets, away to the churchyard. There she saw seated on one of the largest of the gravestones, a ring of Lamias, horrible witches. They put off their rags as if they meant to bathe, and dug down with their long thin fingers into the newly made graves, pulled out the corpses and ate their flesh. Elisa had to pass close by them, and they fastened their dreadful eyes on her, but she prayed her prayer, and gathered the burning nettles and carried them back to the palace.

Only one person had seen her—the Archbishop. He was awake while everyone else was asleep. Now, then, he had found the truth of what he suspected! All was not as it should be with the Queen. She was a witch, and that was how she had corrupted the King and the whole people.

In the confessional he told the King what he had seen and what he feared, and as the cruel words came from his

tongue, the carven images of the saints shook their heads, as if to say: "It is not so; Elisa is innocent." But the Archbishop interpreted it otherwise; he said they were bearing witness against her, shaking their heads at her guilt. Two heavy tears rolled down the King's cheek. He went home with misgiving in his heart, and he feigned to be asleep at night, but no sleep came to his eyes. He saw how Elisa got up, and he saw that she disappeared into her tiny chamber. Day by day his mien grew sadder. Elisa saw it, but did not understand the cause, yet it troubled her and what did she not suffer at heart for her brothers!

70

On the royal velvets and purple her salt tears ran down and lay there like glistening diamonds; while everyone who saw her rich attire wished they were Queen.

Meanwhile she was nearly at the end of her task; only one shirt was still wanting.

But flax she had none, and not a single nettle.

Once again then—only this time— must she go to the churchyard and pluck some handfuls. She thought with horror of the lonely journey and the frightful Lamias, but her will was as steadfast as her trust in God.

Elisa went, but the King and the Archbishop followed. They saw her disappear through the iron gates into the churchyard, and when they neared it, there sat the Lamias upon the gravestones, as Elisa had seen them. And the King turned away, for among them, he thought, was she whose head had that very evening rested on his bosom.

"The people must judge her," said he. And the people did judge her: "She shall be burned in the red fire." From the splendid royal halls she was taken away to a dark vault where the wind whistled through the barred window. In place of velvet and silk they gave her the bundle of nettles she had gathered—she might lay her head on that. The coarse heavy shirts she had woven should be her mattress and coverlets; but nothing dearer to her could they have given her. She began again upon her work and prayed to her God. Outside, the street boys sang mocking ballads about her, and no soul comforted her with a kind word.

Towards evening came the sound of a swan's wing. It was the youngest of the brothers: he had found his sister, and she sobbed aloud with joy, though she knew that the night now coming on was perhaps the last she had to live. But now, too, the work was all but finished, and her brothers were there.

The Archbishop came to pass the last hours with her; he had promised the King that he would. But she shook her head and with look and gesture prayed him to go. That night she must finish her task, or else all would have been in vain—everything—the pain, the tears, the sleepless nights. The Archbishop went away with slanderous words against her, but poor Elisa knew she was guiltless, and went on with her work.

The little mice ran over the floor and dragged the nettles to her feet to help her ever so little; and the thrush perched on the window bar and sang the whole night as gaily as he could, that she might not lose heart.

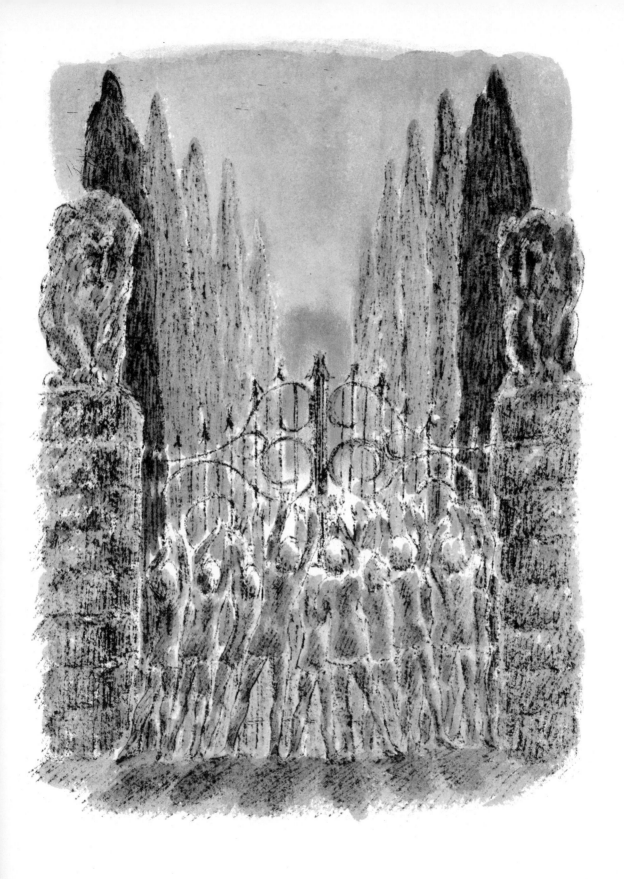

It was still little more than dawn, an hour
before the sun would be up, when the eleven
brothers were at the palace gate, demanding to
be brought to the King. But it could not be,
was the answer; it was still night, the King was
asleep and could not be roused. They besought,
they threatened, the guard came, nay, the King
himself came out and asked what it all meant.
At that instant the sun rose, and there were no
brothers to be seen, but over the palace eleven
wild swans were flying.

75

The whole population came streaming out of the city gates to see the witch burnt. A wretched horse drew the
tumbril in which she sat: they had put on her a kirtle of coarse sackcloth, her beautiful long hair hung loose about her fair head, her cheeks were deathly pale, her lips moved a little, while her fingers twined the green flax. Even on her way to death she did not leave off the work she had begun. Ten of the shirts lay at her feet, and she was working at the eleventh.

The crowd jeered at her. "Look at the witch mumbling there. No hymn book in her hands, no. She's still messing at her foul job. Tear it from her into a thousand shreds." They all crowded in upon her and tried to tear it to bits. But there came eleven swans flying and perched round about her on the tumbril and flapped their great wings. The mob retreated, in terror.

"It's a sign from heaven. Surely she is innocent," many of them whispered; but they dared not say it aloud.

Then the executioner seized her by the hand, but hastily she threw the shirts over the swans—and there stood eleven beautiful princes! But the youngest had one swan's wing instead of an arm, for a sleeve was lacking to his shirt; she had not quite finished it.

"Now I may speak," she said, "I am innocent." And the people who beheld what had come to pass bowed down before her as before a saint. But she sank lifeless into the arms of her brothers, so hardly had the suffering, the fear and the pain weighed upon her.

"Yes, she is innocent," said the eldest brother. And he began to tell all that had befallen. And while he spoke, there spread abroad a perfume as of millions of roses, for every faggot in the pyre had taken root and put forth branches. A fragrant bush stood there, tall and bright with red roses. At its summit was a flower, white and shining, that glistened like a star. The King plucked it and laid it on Elisa's breast, and she awoke with peace and gladness in her heart.

And all the church bells rang out of their own accord,
and the birds came in great flocks, and such a bridal train
80   went back to the palace, as no King yet had ever seen.